D0535194

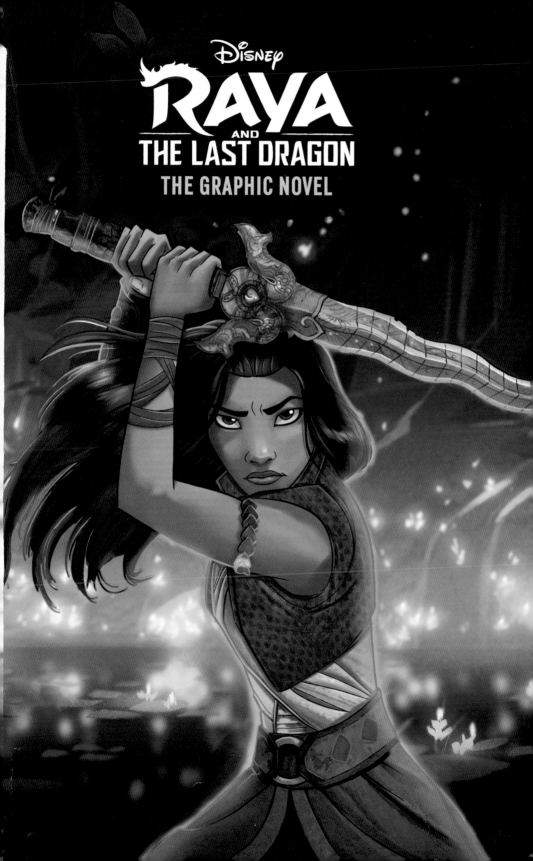

Random House 🏠 New York

Copyright © 2021 Disney Enterprises, Inc. All rights reserved. Published in the United States
by Random House Children's Books, a division of Penguin Random House LLC, 1745 Broadway,
New York, NY 10019, and in Canada by Penguin Random House Canada Limited, Toronto,
in conjunction with Disney Enterprises, Inc. RH Graphic with the book design
is a trademark of Penguin Random House LLC.

rhcbooks.com

ISBN 978-0-7364-4252-7

Printed in the United States of America
10 9 8 7 6 5 4 3 2 1

Raya
AND
THE LAST DRAGON
THE GRAPHIC NOVEL

Random House 🏠 New York

MEET THE CHARACTERS

RAYA

Raya is a proud Guardian of the Dragon Gem, a title she holds alongside her beloved father, Chief Benja of Heart. Her world is turned upside down when the Gem is broken and her father is turned to stone. Now on a mission to save the world, she's grown up to be a resilient warrior whose wit is as sharp as her blade. The only one she trusts is her loyal companion Tuk Tuk.

TUK TUK

Part pill bug, part pug, part high-speed off-road vehicle, and all adorable, Tuk Tuk has been Raya's best friend since she could hold him in the palm of her hand. Now they are both grown, and Tuk Tuk is Raya's faithful, gigantic steed.

SISU

Sisu, short for Sisudatu, is the last dragon of Kumandra. Legends say she's a divine water being of unspeakable beauty and unstoppable magic, but what Raya finds instead is a funny, self-deprecating dragon who sees herself as the perennial C student. Now she must learn to become the dragon of legend if she is to save the world with Raya.

BENJA

Benja is Raya's beloved father and a legendary Guardian of the Dragon Gem known as "the baddest blade in the five lands." As chief of Heart, he's an idealistic and bold visionary who believes that the world is broken because people don't trust each other and who seeks to reunite this fractured world.

NAMAARI

Brilliant, calculating, and a formidable warrior, Namaari is Raya's unrelenting nemesis. She is the daughter of the chief of Fang and is determined to do whatever it takes to protect her people. However, down deep, she holds a secret love for dragons.

BOUN

A precocious street kid
from Tail who's always up
for a business deal, Boun
is an adult in a child's body,
capable and self-sufficient.
He is the self-styled owner,
manager, chef, and captain
of his boat, the *Shrimporium*.
Deep down, he's a vulnerable
child who lost his parents to
the Druun.

TONG

Though Tong still looks like the huge, gruff, fierce Spine warrior he once was, he is now a lonely woodsman after losing his entire village to Druun. With his elevated speech and penchant for watching out for little ones, he is equal parts severity and softness. He is truly a gentle giant.

NOI & THE ONGIS

Part monkey and part catfish, the three Ongis are resourceful con artists from the trading port of Talon. They do everything together, including raise a two-year-old toddler named Noi. She leads their hustle, distracting passersby with her cuteness while the Ongis rob them blind.

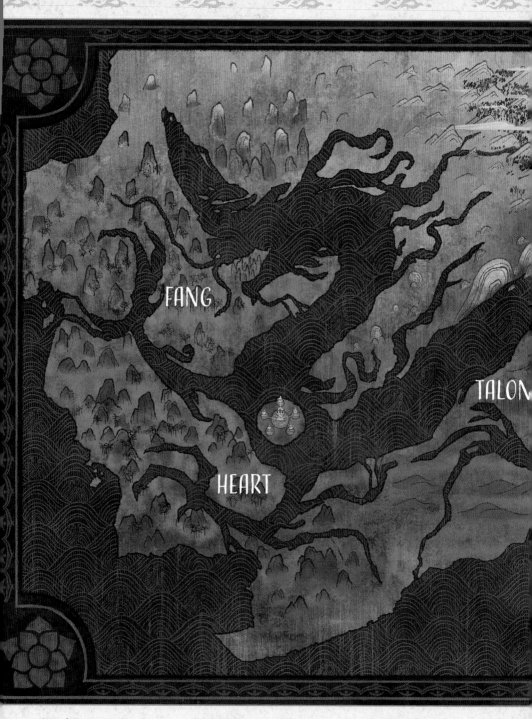

LAND OF KUMANDRA

FANG: Home of Namaari and her mother, Chief Virana, Fang is a nation of fierce warriors and battle cats. Where other clans succumbed to the Druun, Fang thrived with cleverness and determination.

HEART: Home of Raya and Tuk Tuk. Heart is a natural island connected to the rest of the world by the Heart Bridge, built by Chief Benja. This is where the Dragon Gem has been guarded for hundreds of years.

TALON: The center of this land is Talon Port, a market floating on the water. Here, visitors and travelers from the five lands can find food and goods, but also hustlers and con artists.

SPINE: A remote, isolated land, Spine doesn't welcome visitors. Its central fortress is surrounded by walls lined with bamboo spikes and giant snowy mountains.

TAIL: Far from the water, this isolated desert land is where the last dragon found her retreat after she blasted the Druun away. Shipwrecks and the dockyard prove that water once played an essential role in local life.

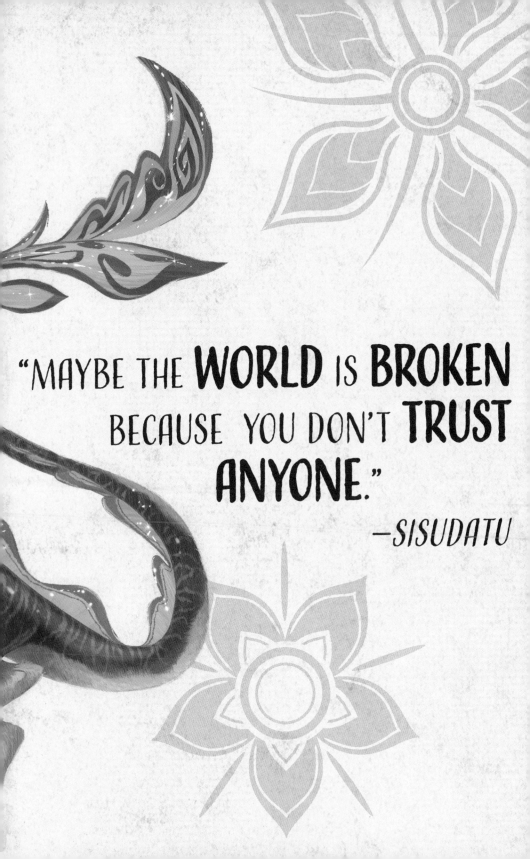

"MAYBE THE **WORLD** IS **BROKEN** BECAUSE YOU DON'T **TRUST ANYONE.**"

—*SISUDATU*

"IT'S NOT ABOUT **MAGIC**. IT'S ABOUT TRUST!"

—RAYA

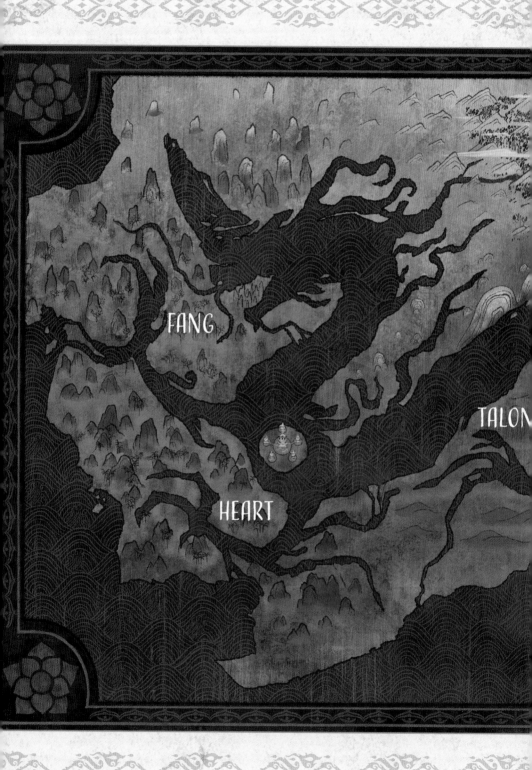

RAYA AND THE LAST DRAGON
THE GRAPHIC NOVEL

SCRIPT ADAPTATION
Alessandro Ferrari

LAYOUT
Otto Schmidt

PENCILS
Otto Schmidt, Arianna Florean,
Andrea Parisi,
Veronica Di Lorenzo

COLORS
Alesia Barsukova,
Watermark Studio (Luigi Aimé,
Lisa Vannini, Samuel Spano)

LETTERING
Edizioni BD

COVER (LAYOUT, INK, COLOR)
Marco Ghiglione

GRAPHIC DESIGN
Red-Spot Srl - Milan, Italy

**DISNEY PUBLISHING
WORLDWIDE**
Global Magazines,
Comics, and Partworks

PUBLISHER
Lynn Waggoner

EDITORIAL TEAM
Bianca Coletti
(Director, Magazines),
Guido Frazzini (Director, Comics),
Carlotta Quattrocolo (Executive Editor),
Stefano Ambrosio (Executive Editor),
Camilla Vedove
(Senior Manager,
Editorial Development),
Behnoosh Khalili (Senior Editor),
Julie Dorris (Senior Editor),
Mina Riazi (Assistant Editor),
Gabriela Capasso (Assistant Editor)

DESIGN
Enrico Soave (Senior Designer)

ART
Ken Shue (VP, Global Art),
Roberto Santillo (Creative Director),
Manny Mederos
(Senior Illustration Manager, Comics),
Marco Ghiglione (Creative Manager),
Stefano Attardi (Illustration Manager)

PORTFOLIO MANAGEMENT
Olivia Ciancarelli (Director)

BUSINESS & MARKETING
Mariantonietta Galla
(Senior Manager, Franchise),
Virpi Korhonen (Editorial Manager)

SPECIAL THANKS
Jeff Clark, Grace Lee, Heather Knowles,
Alison Giordano, Jackson Kaplan,
Osnat Shurer, Paul Felix, Thai Bettistea,
Kaliko Hurley, Leah Latham, Nicole Kim,
Brittany Kikuchi, Maria Elena Naggi